The Runaway Raspberry

Written and Illustrated by Aretha Lane

"The Runaway Raspberry" published through Independent Author Publishing.

Young Author Academy

Dubai, United Arab Emirates

www.youngauthoracademy. com

ISBN: 9798793300032

Printed by Amazon Direct Publishing.

I am an Australian Author also having
written and illustrated 'The Humungus Fungus'
and 'The Evil Weevil'.

I have read a lot of children's books
in the past 12 years,
as I have three boys who love reading,
so I thought it was time to write my own.

There is nothing more magical than holding
and reading a beautiful book.

Based on a true story

In the back of the cold, dark fridge,

at the bottom of the chilly crisper,

was a punnet of red raspberries.

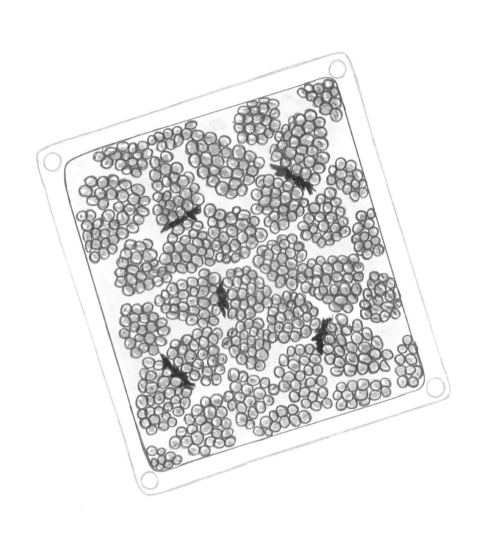

Raspberry
Jam

510g

One particular red raspberry was not very happy being in there, all cold and cramped.

He thought he was in a jam.

He decided to hatch a cunning plan of escape.

He tried to persuade some other raspberries

to break out with him but they thought he was

joking...

"Berry funny," they all said.

He also tried to put the squeeze on the oranges...

The raspberry tried ap'peeling to the bunch of

bananas but they wouldn't split...

He told the pears to come with him

but they wouldn't give in to

'pear pressure'.

He then pressed the grapes until

they started to whine...

He also tried to convince the

coconut but he wouldn't crack...

FRESH SEAL
CRISPER

He soon realised that he would have

to go it alone.

He waited in silence for his escape.

The red raspberry pushed his way to the top of

the punnet pile and as soon as the lid was

removed, he would be ready to jump

as far as he could.

One berry said, "Go, Man'go".

That next day, the whole punnet was lifted out

of the fridge and put on the kitchen bench.

This was his chance.

As soon as that lid was lifted,

he was going to make the leap...

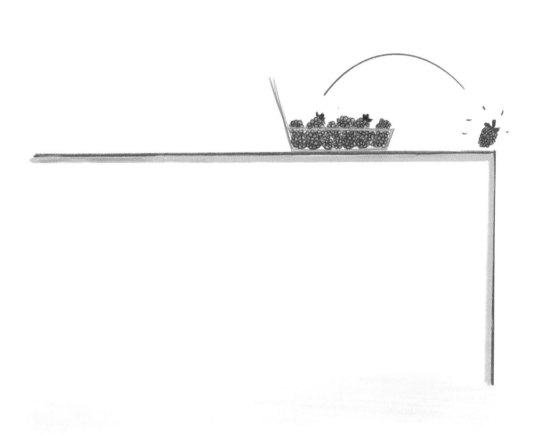

He landed on the edge of the bench, positioned

precariously, balancing on the ledge...

He didn't like it.

He began to panic.

He was all alone.

What had he done?

Nothing could be worse than this.

Nothing!

Then he was eaten.

No raspberries were hurt in the
making of this book.

About the Author
Aretha Lane

Aretha is an Australian Author and mother of three boys, who has written and illustrated a series of fun children's stories.

Aretha has lived in the Middle East for over thirteen years and has wanted to write a series of children's stories that was fun for the child and for the parents reading too.

For Miller, who loves to eat.

FOLLOW ARETHA'S PUBLISHING JOURNEY HERE,

www.youngauthoracademy.com/aretha-lane

www.instagram.com/arethalane_author

SCAN ME

Printed in Great Britain
by Amazon

79669580R00022